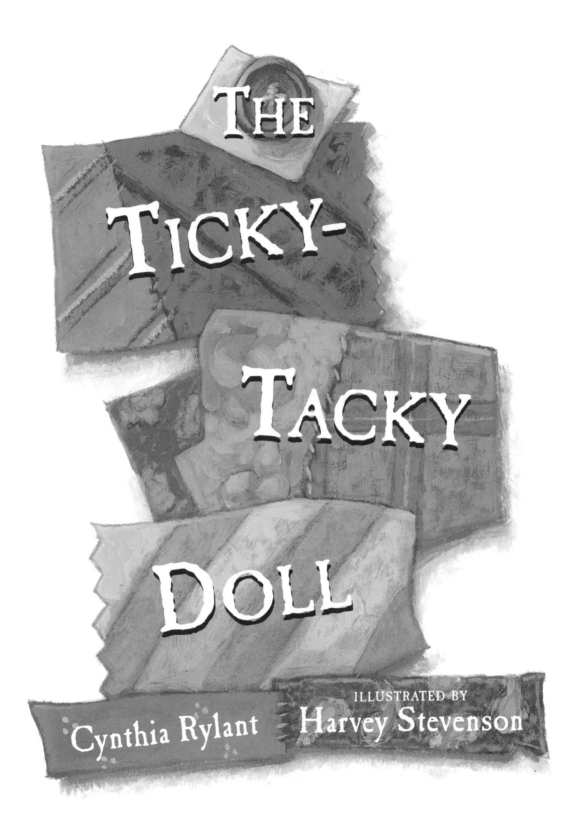

THE TICKY-TACKY DOLL

Cynthia Rylant

ILLUSTRATED BY
Harvey Stevenson

Harcourt, Inc.

San Diego   New York   London

www.HarcourtBooks.com

Library of Congress Cataloging-in-Publication Data
Rylant, Cynthia.
The ticky-tacky doll/Cynthia Rylant; illustrated by Harvey Stevenson.
p.   cm.
Summary: When she has to go to school without her special doll, a
little girl cannot focus on learning her letters and numbers, until her
grandmother realizes what the problem is.
[1. Dolls—Fiction. 2. Schools—Fiction. 3. Grandmothers—Fiction.]
I. Stevenson, Harvey, 1960- ill. I. Title.
PZ7.R982Tj   2002
[E]–dc21   97-20281
ISBN 0-15-201078-5

First edition
H G F E D C B A

Printed in Singapore

The illustrations in this book were painted in acrylics and
Carand'ache crayons on 400 gram Vinci Lavis paper.
The display was set in Caslon Antique.
The text type was set in Saint-Albans.
Color separations by Bright Arts Ltd., Hong Kong
Printed and bound by Tien Wah Press, Singapore
This book was printed on totally chlorine-free Nymolla Art paper.
Production supervision by Sandra Grebenar and Ginger Boyer
Designed by Ivan Holmes

To Grandmama, who sewed for me
—C. R.

For Rebecca Schaffer
—H. S.

Once there was a little girl who owned a ticky-tacky doll. It was ticky, her mother said, because Grandmama had made it from sewing scraps. And it was tacky because pieces of cloth hung from it like soft bits of hair.

The little girl loved her ticky-tacky doll and did not mind its being made from scratch like a buttermilk biscuit. The doll's floppy arms held tight to the little girl's neck on their trips to town. At the supper table the doll fit snugly on the little girl's lap, and its eyes could see what was for dinner.

And at night the doll had a ticky-tacky nightgown to match the one the little girl wore, and the two rested under quilts that reminded them of themselves.

The ticky-tacky doll and the little girl were
always together, season after season, and it seemed
life would go on this way forever. But one day
everything changed, and that was the day the little girl
had to go to school.

There is no place for ticky-tacky dolls in
school. This is very sad, but it is the
way of the world: When children
go to school, toys are left behind.

Well, the little girl might as well have been asked to leave her nose behind, or her two ears, or her eyes. The ticky-tacky doll was as much a part of her as eyes or ears or a nose, and the little girl did not know how else to be.

But she was sent on her first day of school without the ticky-tacky doll anyway, for those were the rules. And the little girl did not eat. And she did not count to ten. Her ticky-tacky doll was at home, watching out the window for her, and knowing this, the little girl had no use for food or numbers.

When she came home, she wrapped the ticky-tacky doll's arms around her neck and held her for a long time.

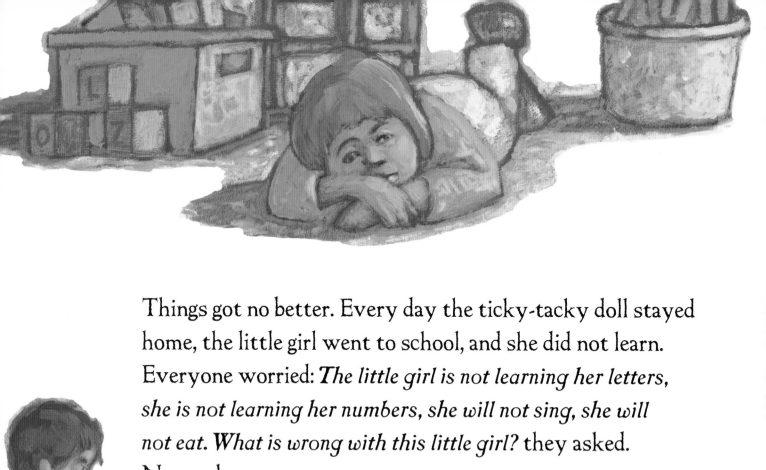

Things got no better. Every day the ticky-tacky doll stayed home, the little girl went to school, and she did not learn. Everyone worried: *The little girl is not learning her letters, she is not learning her numbers, she will not sing, she will not eat. What is wrong with this little girl?* they asked.
No one knew.

But Grandmama knew. Grandmama had been watching. She had seen the sad-eyed little girl walking home from school, had seen her little face brighten like the sun when finally she had the ticky-tacky doll in her arms again. Grandmama had lived a long time and knew about loneliness and missing someone.

Now, the lovely thing about ticky-tacky dolls is that they are always waiting to be made. Anywhere there is a sewing basket, there is a ticky-tacky doll hiding among the scraps.

So, Grandmama made a ticky-tacky child, a child very small and ready to go to school.

Grandmama showed the little girl how nicely the ticky-tacky child fit in the corner of her book bag, how quiet and invisible it could be at school. Grandmama said that the larger ticky-tacky doll would stay behind and watch out the window like all mothers do, waiting for their children to come home.

Every morning after that, the little girl kissed the big
ticky-tacky doll and left her in the window. And she
kissed the ticky-tacky child and took her to school.
She didn't tell anyone the doll was in her book bag and
was learning letters and numbers with her. It was a
secret just for her and Grandmama.

The ticky-tacky child was also given her own
matching nightgown. Every night she slept between
the big ticky-tacky doll and the peaceful little girl,
who now knew so many letters and numbers.

The three would lie warmly under the quilts that reminded them of themselves. And together they would dream all night long . . .

beautiful little scraps and
bits and pieces of dreams.